Taking Care of Mama

Mitra Modarressi

G. P. Putnam's Sons

An Imprint of Penguin Group (US) WITHDRAWN

For Dorri, Taghi and Greg,
who always take such good care of me!

G. P. PUTNAM'S SONS
A division of Penguin Young Readers Group.
Published by The Penguin Group.
Penguin Group (USA) Inc., 375 Hudson Street, New York, NY 10014, U.S.A.
Penguin Group (Canada), 90 Eglinton Avenue East, Suite 700, Toronto, Ontario M4P 2Y3, Canada
(a division of Pearson Penguin Canada Inc.).
Penguin Books Ltd, 80 Strand, London WC2R 0RL, England.
Penguin Ireland, 25 St. Stephen's Green, Dublin 2, Ireland (a division of Penguin Books Ltd.).
Penguin Group (Australia), 250 Camberwell Road, Camberwell, Victoria 3124, Australia (a division of Pearson Australia Group Pty Ltd).
Penguin Books India Pvt Ltd, 11 Community Centre, Panchsheel Park, New Delhi - 110 017, India.
Penguin Group (NZ), 67 Apollo Drive, Rosedale, North Shore 0632, New Zealand (a division of Pearson New Zealand Ltd).
Penguin Books (South Africa) (Pty) Ltd, 24 Sturdee Avenue, Rosebank, Johannesburg 2196, South Africa.
Penguin Books Ltd, Registered Offices: 80 Strand, London WC2R 0RL, England.

Manufactured in China by South China Printing Co. Ltd. Design by Katrina Damkoehler. Text set in Alghera Script.
The art was done in watercolors on Fabriano hot press paper.

Library of Congress Cataloging-in-Publication Data
Modarressi, Mitra.
Taking care of Mama / Mitra Modarressi.   p. cm.
Summary: When Mama gets sick, Papa and the kids wear themselves out doing the cooking and cleaning for the day.
[1. Stories in rhyme. 2. Family life—Fiction. 3. Sick—Fiction. 4. Raccoon—Fiction. 5. Humorous stories.] I. Title.
PZ8.3.M712Tak 2010   [E]—dc22   2009011315

ISBN 978-0-399-25216-7
1 3 5 7 9 10 8 6 4 2

Mama is sick.
What should we do?
　　The thermometer reads
　　One hundred and two.

Papa called the doctor
And the doctor said,
    "Please tell Mama
    To stay in bed!"

"Bed!" said Mama.
"But there's work to do."
"You rest, Mama,
WE'LL take care of YOU!"

We tuck Mama in
And shut the door.

Papa cooks breakfast;
We watch baby Mabel.

It's so much work
Getting food on the table!

Tiptoe, tiptoe,
Is Mama better or worse?
You be the doctor,
And I'll be the nurse.

When lunchtime comes,
We make up a tray:
    Grilled cheese cut in squares—
    Mama likes it that way.

Tiptoe, tiptoe,
Mama's feeling better.
    She wants to get up,
    But we won't let her!

Mabel takes a nap,
And Papa does too.

We pick the carrots
For tonight's veggie stew.

The stew tastes good—
It should be a success.
But then we notice . . .
This house is a mess!

There's no time to waste,
We don't have all day.
If we don't clean up,
What will Mama say?

"I'm really much better,"
Mama calls down.

"We'd better hurry,"
Papa says with a frown.

Tiptoe, tiptoe,
Mama's at the door.
    We've washed the last plate,
    We've swept up the floor.

"My goodness, my dears,"
Mama says with a grin.
"You don't need me at all!
It's as neat as a pin."

"Oh no," we all say
As we slurp up our stew.
"It's really not the same
'Round the house without you."

The End